MANIC PANIC

Laura Shenton

MANIC PANIC

Laura Shenton

Iridescent Toad Publishing

Iridescent Toad Publishing.

Cover by RJ Creatives.

First edition. ISBN 978-1-913779-45-0

Chapter One

The bass pulsed through Jayna's body like an electric current, each beat reverberating against her ribcage as she leaned against the sticky surface of the bar at Voltage. It was the kind of nightclub where the floor clung to shoes with each step, where the air hung heavy with a tangible mixture of cheap vodka, synthetic fog, and raw desperation. Ten o'clock on a Wednesday night, and the place was already a sweaty, writhing mess of bodies pressed together under strobe lights that painted everything in fleeting flashes of neon blue and violent pink. Just how Jayna liked it. Anonymous. Deafeningly loud. A place where she could dissolve into the noise and chaos, disappearing into the crowd and forgetting about the bland walls and steel bars that had kept her contained for the past eighteen months.

She ran a hand through her dark purple hair – freshly dyed just yesterday in the cramped bathroom of her aunt's apartment. The hair dye had been her first purchase after getting out, spending money that could have gone towards more practical necessities. A small rebellion, a visible reclaiming of identity that she wore like a badge. Behind bars at Clearwater, everything had been regulation beige and grey, right down to the dull jumpsuits and the pallid, fluorescent-blanched faces of the other women who'd shared her fate. No means of personal expression allowed. The guards had been particularly vigilant with her, always watching for the telltale shimmer in the air that preceded spellcasting, the subtle movements of fingers weaving unseen energies.

"Another one, please," Jayna shouted at the bartender over the throbbing music, sliding her empty glass forward across the lacquered surface, leaving a trail of condensation in its wake.

The bartender – a lanky guy with sleeve tattoos and gauged ears – nodded without making eye contact, deftly mixing another rum and coke. The ice clinked against the glass as he slid it back to her. Jayna had promised herself she'd go easy tonight, nursing just one or two drinks, but promises were so easy to break when the alternative was sitting alone in her aunt's apartment, drowning in her thoughts and the crushing enormity of readjustment. The parole officer's warning echoed in her mind: "Remember, Jayna, your magic isn't illegal – it's how you use it that matters. One more binding spell on an unwilling person, one more freezing charm without consent, and you're back in for twice as long."

As Jayna fished around in her pocket for a crumpled note to pay for the drink, a woman with bleached blonde hair stumbled clumsily into the narrow space next to her. The woman's sequined top caught the pulsing lights as she jostled Jayna's arm, sloshing sticky, amber liquor onto her hand and the cuff of her leather jacket. Around them, at least a dozen other witches mingled freely in the crowd – Jayna could sense their magical signatures pulsing like faint heartbeats among the chaos, their powers flowing freely and legally as they enhanced their drinks with temperature charms or created small, dazzling light displays for their friends' amusement.

"Watch it," Jayna snapped, wiping her hand vigorously on her black jeans, the liquid leaving a dark stain on the already worn denim. She felt the familiar tingle of her power responding to her irritation, tendrils of arcane energy awakening beneath her skin, eager to be unleashed after months of forced dormancy.

The blonde turned, her mascara smudged beneath glassy, unfocused eyes. Her lips, painted a shimmering shade of peach, twisted into a sneer. "You watch it, bitch. You're hogging the bar. Some of us have been waiting."

Jayna felt the familiar heat rise in her chest, spreading like wildfire through her veins. There was a dangerous tingling in her fingertips that always preceded trouble, a warning sign she'd learnt to recognise all too well. Violet sparks – invisible to normal eyes but blazingly obvious to any witch in the vicinity – began to dance between her knuckles, responding to her rising anger. In prison, surrounded by guards who watched for any sign of magical activity, she'd learnt to control it, to channel it into less destructive outlets – deep breathing, meditation techniques taught by the facility's rehabilitation counsellor. Out here, in the swirling openness of freedom, the old instincts rushed back too easily, like muscle memory that had never really faded.

"Back off," Jayna warned, her voice dropping to a dangerous register that had made cellmates step back during her time inside. Her eyes narrowed as her fingers flexed at her sides, arcane symbols momentarily flickering across her skin – the intricate, ancient patterns of a binding spell forming and dissolving with each heartbeat. The same spell that had frozen that man in place eighteen months ago when he wouldn't take no for an answer. The same spell that the judge had deemed "assault by magical means" despite Jayna's protests that she'd only been defending herself.

"Or what?" The blonde leaned in closer, swaying slightly on her platform heels, her alcohol-sour breath hitting Jayna's face. "You gonna do something about it? In front of all these people?"

The tingling intensified, spreading up from Jayna's fingertips to her wrists. She could feel the energy gathering in her palms, that crackling potential like static electricity before a storm – the same dangerous power that had got her locked up in the first place. One small gesture, barely noticeable in the crowded bar, and this obnoxious woman would freeze where she stood, muscles temporarily paralysed as if struck by an invisible taser. Just for a minute. Just long enough to teach her a lesson about personal space and common courtesy. The incantation – *sistere corpus* – bubbled up in Jayna's mind, ancient Latin words that would channel her innate magical energy into the physical world, bending reality to her will.

Jayna raised her hand slightly, feeling the magic rising within her like mercury in a thermometer, building pressure that begged for release. The familiar words of the incantation danced on the tip of her tongue, ready to be whispered into existence. A faint purple glow emanated from her palms, casting eerie shadows across the blonde's unaware face. It would be so easy – so satisfying... and so similar to what had landed her behind bars for eighteen long months.

Consequences could come later. Right now, all that mattered was the pulsing energy in her veins, the promise of immediate justice, and the sheer temptation to let it all go. The rush of power, the sharp thrill of action. No one was going to mess with her tonight – not after everything she'd been through.

But instead of the release she craved, there was a sudden, violent tug behind her navel, a confusing swirl of light and pressure that compressed her from all sides. The club's thumping music cut out abruptly, replaced by a moment of absolute silence, and then...

Reality fractured around her. Jayna's consciousness split into a kaleidoscope of sensations – her body seeming to exist in multiple places simultaneously, stretched across dimensions in a nauseating smear of perception. Colours inverted, sounds became tastes, and the solid world turned liquid, then gaseous, then something entirely beyond physical states. Her witch's senses, already heightened by the near-casting of her spell, were overwhelmed by the arcane energies ripping her from one location to another. She felt her organs floating independently within her body, her blood momentarily flowing backward through her veins, her nerves firing signals of simultaneous freezing cold and burning heat. The teleportation spell – powerful, urgent, and definitely not of her own casting – pulled her through the fabric of space like a needle through cloth, leaving a trail of psychedelic impressions that would haunt her dreams for weeks.

When the universe reassembled itself around her, she was standing in the middle of her aunt Rachel's living room, still in her clubbing clothes, rum and coke nowhere to be found. The sudden silence was almost as disorientating as the teleportation itself, her ears still ringing with phantom bass notes. Her stomach lurched violently, the magical whiplash of forced teleportation making her sway on her feet as sparks of residual energy cascaded from her skin like purple snowflakes, dissipating into the mundane air of her aunt's apartment. The taste of ozone and mildew – the unmistakable signature of emergency summoning magic – lingered on her tongue, a bitter reminder that someone, somewhere, had deemed this interruption necessary.

"Seriously?" Jayna groaned, stumbling slightly as she regained her balance on the faded Persian rug her aunt had owned for as long as she could remember. The familiar scent of herbs and old books overwhelmed her as she tried to get her bearings.

Rachel sat calmly on the worn leather sofa, a thick, ancient-looking book with a cracked spine in her lap and a cup of herbal tea steaming on the coffee table beside a small dish of crystals. Her dark hair was pulled back in a loose bun, silver strands catching the warm light from the standing lamp beside her. She raised an eyebrow at Jayna, looking completely unsurprised by her sudden materialisation in the middle of the living room.

"Good evening to you too," Rachel said mildly, placing a pressed flower bookmark between the pages to mark her place. "I thought you might appreciate the lift home. That club looked like it was getting a bit... intense."

Jayna scowled, crossing her arms defensively across her chest. "I was handling it."

"Yes, I could see that," Rachel replied, her tone neutral but her eyes knowing. "You were handling it exactly the way that got you eighteen months in Clearwater Correctional. That blonde girl wouldn't have known what hit her."

The anger that had been building inside Jayna flickered uncertainly like a candle in a draft, unsteady and fading. "You were spying on me?" she demanded, though the accusation sounded hollow even to her own ears.

Rachel sighed, the sound soft and tired. She removed her reading glasses and placed them on the coffee table next to her tea. "I wasn't spying, Jayna. I was checking in. There's a difference." She tapped her temple with a finger adorned with several silver rings. "The visions come whether I want them to or not. You know that. And lucky for you, I saw one right before you were about to make a very bad decision."

Jayna wanted to argue, to demand to be taken back to the club, to insist that she was twenty-four years old and an adult who could make her own choices, magical or otherwise.

But the fight drained out of her as quickly as it had come, leaving behind exhaustion and a dull headache forming at her temples. She slumped onto the overstuffed armchair opposite her aunt, kicking off her scuffed combat boots with twin thuds against the hardwood floor.

"I wasn't going to hurt her," Jayna muttered, picking at a loose thread on the chair's arm. "Just... scare her a little. Teach her some manners."

"And how would that have worked out for your parole?" Rachel asked gently, no judgment in her voice, only concern that made Jayna feel worse than any lecture could have.

Jayna closed her eyes, feeling the last of the magical energy dissipate from her fingertips, leaving them cold and slightly numb. Her parole officer, Ms Winters – a stern woman with silver-rimmed glasses and a perpetual clipboard – had been crystal clear during their meeting last Monday: one slip-up, one hint of magical misconduct, one complaint about unexplained phenomena in her vicinity, and she'd be back behind bars faster than she could say "second chance".

"I know," Jayna admitted reluctantly, the words feeling like gravel in her throat. "You're right."

Rachel's expression softened, crow's feet crinkling at the corners of her eyes. She stood up, the leather sofa creaking with the movement, and went to the kitchen. The sounds of a refrigerator opening, a plate being set down, butter sizzling in a pan drifted through the archway. She returned a moment later with a plate that held a perfectly grilled cheese sandwich, golden-brown and cut diagonally the way Jayna had always preferred since childhood.

"I figured you might be hungry," Rachel said, setting the plate down in front of her niece. "Alcohol on an empty stomach never leads to good decisions."

Despite herself, Jayna's stomach growled audibly, reminding her that she hadn't eaten since the bland turkey sandwich she'd had for lunch. "Thanks," she mumbled, picking up half the sandwich. The first bite was perfect – crispy bread with just the right amount of butter, cheese melted to the ideal consistency, a hint of the fancy stone-ground mustard Rachel always used. It tasted like childhood, like the days before her powers had manifested, before everything had become so complicated.

They sat in comfortable silence as Jayna ate, the only sounds the ticking of the antique clock on the mantel and the occasional turning of pages as Rachel returned to her book. When Jayna finished, brushing crumbs from her fingers, Rachel pushed a cup of tea across the table without looking up from her reading.

"Chamomile with a touch of lavender and valerian root," she said. "Good for calming the nerves. Better than whatever they were serving at that club."

Jayna took a sip, the warmth spreading through her chest and settling some of the residual agitation from the night's events. "I'm trying, you know," she said finally, staring into the pale golden liquid. "It's just... harder than I thought it would be. Being out."

"I know you are," Rachel replied, looking up to meet her niece's eyes. "Nobody expects you to have it all figured out right away. Especially not me."

"Everything's different now. The world kept spinning while I was locked up. And yet it's all the same, somehow. Like I'm the one who's changed but also stayed exactly as I was. Does that make sense?"

Rachel nodded, her eyes reflecting understanding that came from her own troubled past. "Perfect sense. You're different, but the world didn't wait for you while you were gone. It never does. That's the disorientating part of coming back."

Jayna twisted the silver ring on her middle finger – a gift of commitment from Claire when they were inside together. Simple, slightly tarnished, with a small amethyst that matched the purple of her hair. "I miss her," she said quietly, the vulnerable admission hanging in the air between them.

"I know you do, honey. But she'll be out soon. Eight more months, right?" Rachel leaned forward, her voice gentle.

"Two hundred and forty-three days," Jayna corrected automatically. She had vowed to count each passing day religiously, to mark them with a small X on the calendar that hung in her bedroom.

Rachel reached across and squeezed Jayna's hand, her skin warm from holding the teacup. "One day at a time, remember? That's how you got through before. That's how you'll get through now."

Jayna nodded, feeling the knot in her chest loosen slightly under her aunt's understanding. She glanced around the small apartment – mismatched furniture collected over decades, shelves crowded with Rachel's ever-growing collection of strange artefacts and ancient spell books, dried herbs hanging in bunches from the kitchen doorway, the lingering smell of incense and sage that had permeated the very walls. It wasn't much, but it was more of a home than she'd had in years.

"I really would have regretted it," Jayna admitted after a long pause, running her finger around the rim of the teacup. "Using magic on that woman. It wouldn't have been worth it. Not after everything."

"No," Rachel agreed, tucking a stray strand of hair behind her ear. "It wouldn't have. The moment of satisfaction never outweighs the consequences. That's something I had to learn the hard way too."

"So... thanks. For the timely extraction. Even if your teleportation spells still make me want to throw up afterwards." Jayna attempted a weak smile.

Rachel returned the smile, her face crinkling endearingly. "That's what aunts are for. Especially witch aunts with inconvenient prophetic visions. And I've been working on making the landings smoother, but instantaneous spatial displacement is tricky business."

Jayna's smile strengthened, small but genuine as her tension began to ebb away. "Got any ice cream? Near-magical misdemeanours always make me crave something sweet."

"Rocky road in the freezer. Your favourite. I stocked up when I knew you were coming home." Rachel stood, her joints cracking slightly. "And maybe tomorrow we can work on some grounding exercises. Ways to channel that energy when you feel it building up."

As Rachel went to get the ice cream, Jayna leaned back in the chair, feeling the last of the night's adrenaline drain away. Maybe tonight wasn't a total loss after all. A lesson learnt without consequences, which was more than she could say for most of her life's decisions. And in two weeks' time she could visit Claire during afternoon visiting hours, share stories about the outside world, remind her that there was an after to all of this. The thought warmed her more than the tea.

Two hundred and forty-three days. They could make it. One day at a time.

Chapter Two

Clearwater Correctional's drab visitation room hadn't changed since Jayna had last sat there as an inmate. The same flickering fluorescent lights buzzed overhead. The same uncomfortable plastic chairs – moulded in a shape that somehow managed to fit no human body comfortably – were arranged in neat rows. The same faded inspirational posters clung stubbornly to beige walls, their once-bright colours now muted by years of institutional lighting. Even the smell was the same – industrial cleaning products failing to mask the underlying scent of too many bodies in too small a space, with notes of instant coffee and the faint metallic tang of anxiety that seemed to permeate every crevice.

Jayna sat at the small table, her legs bouncing unconsciously as she waited, her fingers drumming a silent rhythm against her thighs. She'd dressed carefully that morning – black jeans without any rips, a dark purple blouse that Rachel had ironed for her until every crease was perfect, her silver ring polished to a shine that caught the harsh overhead lights. Her red lipstick felt like armour, a declaration that the woman who had left these walls was not the same one who had entered them as in inmate.

When the door on the opposite side of the room finally opened with its familiar hydraulic hiss, Jayna's heart jumped into her throat, her pulse skittering like a startled animal.

Claire walked in, escorted by a guard whose expression suggested he'd rather be somewhere else. Her prison uniform hung loose on her frame – she'd lost weight since Jayna had last seen her, the grey fabric bunching unflatteringly at her waist where it had once fitted snugly. Her brown hair was pulled back in a practical ponytail, revealing the sharp angles of her cheekbones, now more pronounced than before. There were shadows under her eyes that hadn't been there before, purplish crescents that spoke of restless nights on a thin mattress.

When she spotted Jayna, her face transformed, lighting up with a smile that made Jayna's chest ache with a familiar, bittersweet pressure.

"Hey, troublemaker," Claire said as she sat down across from Jayna, the plastic chair creaking beneath her enthusiasm.

"Hey, yourself," Jayna replied, fighting the urge to reach across and touch Claire's face, to trace the new hollows of her cheeks, knowing the guards would shut that down immediately. "You look good."

Claire snorted, the sound both familiar and endearing. "Liar. I look like warmed-over crap and we both know it." She leaned in slightly, her voice dropping to a conspiratorial whisper. "But you... Damn, girl! Freedom looks good on you. Love the hair."

Jayna self-consciously touched her purple locks, still unused to the vibrant colour after her prison-regulated appearance. "Yeah? Not too much?"

"Never too much," Claire said reassuringly, her voice softening to that tone she reserved only for Jayna, the one that made even the most hardened inmates turn away to give them privacy. "It's just so... you. The real you."

Their eyes held for a long moment, a thousand unspoken words passing between them in that silent language they'd developed over shared meals and meaningful gazes after lights out. Then Claire leaned back, her tough exterior sliding back into place like a well-worn jacket, protection against the harsh realities of their surroundings.

"So, tell me everything," Claire commanded, crossing her arms over her chest, the grey fabric crinkling. "What's life like on the outside? Is Rachel driving you nuts yet with all her mystical mumbo-jumbo?"

Jayna laughed, the sound echoing slightly in the acoustically challenged room. "Rachel's been great, actually. Saved my arse when I nearly did something monumentally stupid."

Claire raised an eyebrow, interest sparking in her eyes. "Oh yeah? What kind of trouble are you getting into without me there to be your impulse control?"

Jayna recounted the nightclub incident in vivid detail. She watched Claire's expressions shift from amusement to concern and back again, like clouds passing over the sun.

"So she just... poofed you home with her freaky magic stuff? Man, I wish I could have seen your face when you realised what was happening," Claire said, the corner of her mouth lifting in that endearing half-smile.

"It wasn't my finest moment," Jayna admitted, rubbing the back of her neck where tension still lingered. "But she was right. One wrong move and..." She gestured around the visitation room, at the guards positioned at regular intervals, at the cameras monitoring their every movement.

"And you'd be right back here with me," Claire finished, the lightness in her voice not quite matching her expression. "Which, selfishly, I wouldn't hate. But I'm glad Rachel's looking out for you." Her voice grew serious, the playfulness dropping away. "You've got to be careful, Jay. I mean it. I can't stand the thought of you ending up back in here, watching all that progress slip away."

"I know, I know. I'm trying." Jayna fidgeted with her ring, spinning it around her finger in that nervous gesture Claire had always found cute. "It's just... everything out there feels so loud and fast and overwhelming. Like someone cranked up the volume on the whole world while I was in here. And I keep waiting for it to feel normal again, but it doesn't. Not yet, anyway."

Claire nodded, absorbing the words. "It'll get there. Just takes time. Remember how weird it felt when you arrived here at the start of your sentence? How everything seemed to move in slow motion? It's like that, but in reverse."

"How are things in here?" Jayna asked, changing the subject, her eyes scanning Claire's face for signs of what wasn't being said.

Claire rolled her eyes, the gesture so familiar it made Jayna's heart constrict. "Martinez got transferred to maximum security last week, after that business with the toothbrush shank. Now there's this new girl, Dawson, trying to prove how tough she is by picking fights with anyone who's been here longer than six months." She shrugged one shoulder dismissively. "Nothing I can't handle. You know me – I've always been good at managing difficult personalities."

But Jayna caught the slight wince as Claire moved, the careful way she held her left side, the almost imperceptible tightening around her eyes that signalled pain. "What happened? And don't bother lying to me, I can tell when you're hurting. I always could."

Claire's expression closed off for a moment, shutters coming down over her expressive eyes, then softened under Jayna's persistent gaze. "It's nothing serious. Just a little disagreement in the yard yesterday about who had dibs on the weight bench."

"Claire..."

"It's handled, ok?" Claire cut her off, a note of steel entering her voice. "I'm fine. Really." She reached across the table, their fingertips touching briefly before she pulled back, both of them aware of the guard's watchful gaze.

"Don't worry about me. I've survived in here so far. Eight more months is nothing."

"Two hundred and twenty-nine days," Jayna corrected, the number burned into her consciousness like a brand.

Claire's smile turned tender, the hardness melting away. "You're still counting down?"

"Every day," Jayna replied, her voice catching slightly. "I mark my calendar every morning, first thing."

"Me too," Claire admitted. "Well, not a real calendar. I've got hash marks on the wall behind my bed. Old school, but it works." She hesitated, then asked, "You been looking for work like we talked about?"

Jayna shifted uncomfortably, the plastic chair squeaking beneath her. "Sort of. I had an interview at that coffee shop on Belmont yesterday, the one with the blue awning and the weird latte art."

"And?" Claire prompted, leaning forward slightly.

"And they said they'd call me back, but the manager kept looking at me like I might steal the espresso machine or start dealing beans out the back door." Jayna shrugged, trying to appear more nonchalant than she felt. "There's another place, a bookstore, that's hiring. Rachel knows the owner from some metaphysical book club or something. I'm going to try there next week."

Claire nodded encouragingly, her eyes lighting up. "That sounds perfect for you. Remember how you used to read to me at night when they finally turned the lights out, and we'd huddle under that thin blanket with our tiny book light?"

Jayna smiled at the memory – she had whispered passages from whatever paperback they'd managed to borrow from the prison library, their cellmate pretending to be annoyed but secretly listening too.

"I still have that copy of *Little Women* you gave me," Claire said, the softness entering her voice that few people ever got to hear. "The one with all your notes in the margins and the coffee stain on page twenty-four."

"You'd better be taking good care of it," Jayna warned, only half-joking.

"Of course I am. It's my most prized possession in this place. I keep it wrapped in my cleanest t-shirt." Claire leaned forward, lowering her voice to avoid being overheard by the nearest guard. "I read it when I can't sleep, which is most nights lately. Makes me feel like you're still here, reading to me."

Jayna swallowed hard against the sudden tightness in her throat, blinking rapidly to dispel the tears gathering in her eyes. "I miss that too."

"Two hundred and twenty-nine days," Claire repeated, like a mantra, a promise. "We can do this."

The guard called out a ten-minute warning, his voice echoing in the sterile room. Claire glanced at the clock mounted on the wall, its second hand ticking away their precious time together, her tough façade slipping just a fraction to reveal the vulnerability underneath.

"Tell me what you're going to do when you get out," Jayna said quickly, wanting to see Claire smile again, to erase that momentary flash of fear. "First thing. The very first."

Claire's eyes lit up, focusing on the future instead of the present. "First thing? I'm going to take the longest, hottest shower in the history of showers. With actual water pressure that doesn't feel like someone spitting on you from six feet away. And shampoo that doesn't smell like industrial cleaner mixed with disappointment."

"And then?" Jayna prompted, grinning.

"And then I'm going to eat a massive bacon cheeseburger from Eddie's, with those sweet potato fries I'm always talking about. And a chocolate milkshake so thick you need a spoon to start it."

Jayna laughed, picturing it clearly. "And then?"

Claire's voice dropped, her eyes holding Jayna's with an intensity that seemed to make the rest of the room fade away. "And then I'm going to kiss you until neither of us can breathe. Until I forget what it's like to be anywhere but with you."

The air between them seemed to crackle with electricity, not unlike the feeling of magic gathering in Jayna's fingertips when she practised her craft, but warmer, deeper, more fundamental – like the difference between a spark and a flame.

"I'll hold you to that," Jayna murmured.

"You'd better."

The final warning came too soon, slicing through their moment like a knife.

As Claire stood to leave, she hesitated, glancing at the guard who was already moving towards them with routine efficiency, then quickly whispered while she still had the chance, "I'm working on something in here, Jay. Something big. For us. For after."

Jayna frowned, alarm bells ringing in the back of her mind. "What do you mean? What kind of something?"

But Claire was already backing away as the guard approached. "Trust me," she called to Jayna, making it sound entirely innocent. "I've got plans. Two hundred and twenty-nine days, and then it's you and me. Just like we talked about."

Before Jayna could respond, Claire was being led through the door, throwing one last smile over her shoulder before disappearing from view. The door closed behind her with a cruel hiss that seemed to punctuate the finality of their parting.

As Jayna collected her belongings from the security desk and made her way out of the correctional facility, passing through the series of electronically locked doors that separated the imprisoned from the free, she couldn't shake the sense of unease that settled in her stomach like a cold stone. Claire had never been one for impulse control – it was what made her so loveable, that live-wire spontaneity, that refusal to be contained by other people's expectations, but it was also what had landed them both in trouble more than once.

Outside, the air felt fresh after the stifling atmosphere of the prison, carrying the scent of newly cut grass and distant rain clouds. Jayna took a deep breath, filling her lungs completely in a way that still felt like a luxury, trying to push away her worry. Claire was smart. Claire was resourceful. Claire could take care of herself, had proven that time and again. But still...

She pulled out her phone – another novelty that hadn't quite lost its shine – and texted Rachel: *Visit done. Heading home now. Can we talk when I'm back?*

The response came almost immediately, as if Rachel had been waiting with her phone in hand: *Of course. Making your favourite lasagne with the good cheese. Pick up garlic bread on your way? And maybe some salad?*

Jayna smiled despite herself, some of the tension easing from her shoulders. Rachel always knew, somehow, what she needed – even before she herself did. Maybe that was just part of her aunt being a seer, of having that connection to patterns and possibilities that others couldn't perceive. Or maybe it was because she was family – the real kind, born not just of blood, but choice.

Will do, Jayna texted back, and headed for the bus stop, her thoughts still tangled around Claire's cryptic words and the countdown that seemed simultaneously too long and not long enough.

Two hundred and twenty-nine days. What kind of plans did Claire have? And would they lead to a new beginning – or just more trouble?

Chapter Three

The bookstore smelt of paper, dust, and the faint hint of coffee. Sunlight slanted through the tall windows, catching dust motes that danced in golden beams across the wooden floorboards. Jayna stood behind the counter, carefully placing price stickers on a stack of used paperbacks. Her fingers worked methodically, peeling each small circular sticker and pressing it gently onto the inside cover of each book. Three weeks into her new job at Arcane Affairs Bookshop, and she was finally starting to feel like she belonged among its towering shelves.

"You're getting faster at that," observed Eliza, the owner, a grey-haired woman with kind eyes behind glasses perched on her nose. She leaned against the counter, her cardigan the colour of faded roses.

Jayna smiled, smoothing down a sticker with her thumb. She didn't mention that in prison, any task – no matter how mundane – had been a welcome distraction from the endless hours of confinement. The repetitive nature of pricing books was almost soothing, giving her mind space to wander while her hands stayed busy. "Thanks again for giving me a chance, Eliza. I know Rachel probably twisted your arm..."

Eliza waved dismissively, silver bangles jingling softly on her wrist. "Rachel suggested, she didn't twist. And you've proven her right." She adjusted her glasses and gave Jayna an appraising look. "You've got a good eye for books, and customers like you." She lowered her voice conspiratorially, leaning in closer so that Jayna could smell her lavender perfume. "Especially that university boy who keeps coming in during your shifts to browse the poetry section. The one with the tweed jacket and those earnest eyes."

Jayna laughed, a sound that still sometimes surprised her with its freedom. "Tristan? He's just really into Sylvia Plath. He's writing his thesis on female poets of the twentieth century." She remembered his passionate rambling about *Lady Lazarus* last week, how his hands had gestured wildly as he spoke.

"Mmm-hmm. And I'm just really into inventory spreadsheets." Eliza gathered up some books to re-shelf, balancing the stack against her hip with familiar ease. "You're allowed to flirt, you know. Being loyal doesn't mean you can't have a little fun. A little conversation never hurt anyone."

"I'm not interested," Jayna said firmly, feeling the familiar weight of Claire's silver ring on her finger. She twisted it absently, a habit she'd developed. "I'm just... waiting."

Eliza's expression softened, crow's feet deepening around her eyes. "Rachel mentioned your girlfriend. Claire, right? When's she getting out?"

"Two hundred and four days," Jayna answered automatically, the number etched into her consciousness like a countdown clock she couldn't turn off.

"Well, she's a lucky woman to have someone so devoted," Eliza said, patting Jayna's arm before heading to the back of the store, her footsteps creaking on the old floorboards.

Jayna continued pricing books, her thoughts drifting reliably to Claire, when the bell above the door jingled – a bright, clear sound that interrupted her reverie. She looked up to see Rachel entering, carrying two takeout cups from the café across the street. Her aunt's hair was windblown, and her smile was warm but tinged with something Jayna recognised immediately – concern.

"Thought you might need an afternoon pick-me-up," Rachel said, placing one of the cups – an iced latte with an extra shot, Jayna's favourite – on the counter. The condensation from the cold cup formed a small ring on the wooden surface.

"You're a lifesaver," Jayna said, taking a long sip, the coffee bitter and sweet on her tongue. "What brings you to this side of the city? Besides caffeinating your favourite niece?"

Rachel shrugged, leaning against the counter, her bangles clinking against the wood. "Can't an aunt check in on her niece's new job? See how she's settling in? Maybe browse the new releases while I'm here?"

Jayna gave her a knowing look. "You had a vision, didn't you?" She kept her voice low, though the store was empty save for an elderly man browsing the military history section, his hearing aid visible. "What, am I going to mess up the register? Accidentally sell a first edition for the price of an average paperback?"

"Nothing like that," Rachel assured her, her eyes steady and serious. "I just… had a feeling you might need to talk."

Jayna studied her aunt's face, noting the slight furrow between her brows that appeared when she was troubled. Rachel had never been one to abuse her seer abilities for trivial matters. If she was here, there was a reason – and judging by the tightness around her eyes, not a happy one.

"Is it about Claire?" Jayna asked, lowering her voice further, feeling her heart rate quicken slightly.

Rachel hesitated, tapping a fingernail against her paper cup. "Partially. And partially about you." She glanced around the store, at the shelves of books standing like sentinels. "Can you take a break?"

Jayna checked the time on the vintage clock that hung above the register. "Eliza's in the back. I can step outside for a few minutes." She raised her voice slightly, calling towards the back room. "Eliza? I'm stepping out front for just a moment. I'll be right outside if anyone needs help."

A muffled affirmative came from the back, and Jayna grabbed her coffee before following Rachel outside.

They moved to the small bench outside the bookstore, beneath the faded green awning that provided a slice of shade against the afternoon sun. Jayna fidgeted with the straw in her drink, poking it through the ice cubes, the plastic making a soft crackling sound. "So? What's going on?"

Rachel took a deep breath, her shoulders rising and falling. "I've been seeing... fragments. Nothing concrete, just flashes. You, unhappy. Claire, making choices that put you both at risk." She stared into her coffee cup as if searching for more answers among the cream swirls.

Jayna frowned, a cold feeling settling in her stomach despite the warmth of the day.

"What kind of choices? Is she in danger?" Her fingers tightened around her cup, making the ice shift.

"Not exactly. But I'm concerned about the path she's on." Rachel placed a hand on Jayna's knee, her touch gentle but firm. "Has she mentioned anything unusual to you? Plans for when she gets out that seem… impractical? Things that sound too good to be true?"

Jayna thought about Claire's cryptic comments, the ones she had urgently slipped in towards the end of visiting time. "She mentioned having plans for us but didn't elaborate."

Rachel nodded, as if this confirmed something, her lips pressing together in a thin line. "Jayna, I know you love her. And I know the waiting is hard. But I need you to promise me something." A light breeze ruffled her hair, carrying the scent of fresh bread from the bakery down the street.

"What?" Jayna asked, her voice coming out sharper than she intended.

"Promise me you'll think carefully before agreeing to anything Claire suggests. Especially if it involves..." Rachel hesitated, choosing her words with obvious care. "Shortcuts. Quick money. Anything that sounds too easy or too good to be true."

Jayna stiffened, her back straightening against the bench. "What's that supposed to mean? You don't even know her." The familiar heat of defensiveness rose in her chest, spreading outward.

"I know you," Rachel countered gently, her eyes soft with concern. "And I know how much you've worked to get where you are now. This job, your parole compliance, the therapy sessions – you're building something real. Something sustainable. Something that can last."

"And you think Claire will ruin that?" Jayna could feel her temper rising, the familiar tingle in her fingertips that signalled her magic responding to her emotions. She curled her hands into fists, focusing on the feeling of her nails against her palms, using the small pain as an anchor.

"I think Claire has her own journey," Rachel said carefully, her voice measured. "And right now, she's still inside those walls, thinking like someone who's inside. That survival mindset, that focus on the immediate. But you're out here, Jayna. You're starting to see beyond the next day, the next week. You're planning a future."

Jayna wanted to argue, to defend Claire, but something in Rachel's words resonated uncomfortably. The silver ring felt suddenly heavy on her finger.

"I love her," Jayna said, her voice small, the words hanging in the air between them.

"I know you do. And that doesn't have to change. But love doesn't mean following someone down a dangerous path." Rachel squeezed Jayna's knee gently. "Love sometimes means being strong enough to show someone a better way."

Jayna looked down at her hands, at the silver ring that meant so much to her. The small amethyst stone caught the light. "Two hundred and four days is a long time."

"It's also a gift," Rachel said, her voice gentle but firm. "Time for you to figure out what you want, what kind of life you're building. So that when Claire does get out, you can help her see the possibilities, instead of her pulling you back into old patterns."

The bell over the bookstore door jingled as a customer walked in, the sound bright in the afternoon quiet. Jayna stood up. "I should get back."

Rachel rose as well, giving Jayna a quick hug, her arms strong and comforting. "Think about what I said. And remember, your choices are your own. Your magic, your heart, your future – they belong to you, not to anyone else."

As Jayna watched her aunt walk away, she felt torn between loyalty to Claire and the uncomfortable truth in Rachel's words. She loved Claire – fierce, impulsive, loyal Claire with her quick smile and quicker temper – but she also loved the simple, steady life she was beginning to build for herself. The quiet satisfaction of a day's work at the bookstore. The peace of coming home to Rachel's apartment, of cooking dinner together, of belonging somewhere without the constant threat of discovery or disaster.

Could she have both? Or would she eventually have to choose?

52

Chapter Four

"Do you think we're just kidding ourselves?" Claire asked, her voice flat and devoid of its usual warmth, the fluorescent lights of the visitation room casting an unflattering sheen across her face.

Jayna stared at her across the small table, caught off guard by the question that had seemed to come out of nowhere. It had been a strained visit from the start – tension hanging in the air like an approaching storm. Claire had arrived late, distracted, with a new hardness in her eyes that Jayna had never seen before – a defensive shell that hadn't been there during their last visit.

"What do you mean?" Jayna asked, though a cold dread was already settling in her stomach. She clasped her hands together to stop them from trembling.

Claire gestured vaguely between them. "This. Us. The whole "wait for me, we'll be together" thing. It's been three months since you got out. You've got a job now, a life. Maybe we should just…"

"Just what?" Jayna demanded, louder than she intended. A guard with tired eyes glanced their way from his position by the door, and she lowered her voice to a harsh whisper. "Just give up? Is that what you want? After everything we've been through together?"

Claire wouldn't meet her eyes, focusing instead on a scuff mark on the table between them. "I want you to be happy, Jay. And I'm starting to think maybe that doesn't include waiting around for an ex-con with nothing to offer but baggage and bad memories."

"That's bull," Jayna protested, feeling heat rising to her cheeks. "Where is this coming from? When I spoke to you on the phone we were talking about our plans, our future – that apartment we wanted near the park, the second-hand furniture we'd find. Now suddenly you're writing us off like we're nothing?"

Claire's jaw tightened, her muscles clenching visibly beneath her skin. "I'm being realistic. Relationships that start in here don't usually make it out there. That's just statistics, not sentiment. We both know that."

"So all those promises, all those plans – that was just prison talk? Something to pass the time while we served our sentences?" Jayna could feel her magic stirring beneath her skin, responding to her anger and hurt. She had to force it down, focusing on keeping her voice steady despite the turmoil raging inside.

"No, it wasn't…" Claire started, then stopped, sighing heavily, her shoulders slumping under an invisible weight. "I've just been doing a lot of thinking, that's all. Lying awake at night, staring at the ceiling, wondering if we were just holding on to a dream that can't survive in reality."

Jayna leaned forward, the hard chair uncomfortable against her thighs, trying to catch Claire's gaze with an intensity that demanded acknowledgment. "Talk to me. What's really going on? This isn't like you – to just give up without a fight."

For a moment, Claire's tough exterior cracked like thin ice, revealing a glimpse of vulnerability underneath – the Claire that Jayna had fallen in love with during those long nights of whispered confidences. "You got that bookstore job – the one with the nice owner who doesn't care about your record. You're living with your aunt in that nice part of the city with the coffee shops and the farmers' market. You're doing well, Jayna. Really well."

"And that's... bad?" Jayna asked, confusion threading through her words.

"No, it's great. It's what you deserve." Claire finally looked up, her eyes suspiciously bright in the harsh institutional lighting. "But let's be real. When I get out, what am I bringing to the table? No skills that matter on the outside, no prospects, just a record and a bad attitude that I've spent years perfecting. I've got nothing but empty pockets and a reputation that follows me like a shadow."

Understanding dawned on Jayna, washing over her like cold water. "You think you'll hold me back – that I'll be better off without you."

Claire shrugged, but the gesture wasn't as casual as she clearly wanted it to be – too much tension in her shoulders, too much pain in her eyes. "Your aunt thinks so. I'd bet my commissary on it."

Jayna blinked, thrown by the unexpected mention. "What? Rachel has never even met you. She doesn't even know you beyond what I've told her."

"No, but I bet she's told you to be careful. To think twice before hitching your chances to mine once I'm out." Claire's bitter smile confirmed that Jayna's expression had given away the truth. "Yeah, that's what I thought. Your face says it all, Jay. Always has."

"It's not like that," Jayna protested, hearing the weakness in her own argument. "Rachel is just… protective. She's been looking out for me since I was a kid. She has these visions sometimes…"

"Visions," Claire echoed mockingly, her eyebrows rising. "Right. Conveniently telling her that poor rough Claire with her bad history and worse prospects is going to ruin precious Jayna's second chance at a normal life. How incredibly fortunate."

Anger flared in Jayna like a struck match. "That's not fair. To Rachel or to me. I've defended you. I've told her how much you mean to me, how we're going to make it work against all odds. I've fought for us."

"And has she believed you?" Claire challenged, leaning forward now, intensity radiating from her like heat. "Or does she just nod and smile and keep dropping little hints about how you could do better? How there are other fish in the sea – ones without criminal records and anger management issues?"

Jayna opened her mouth to argue, then closed it again, the words dying on her lips. The truth was, since their big talk that day outside the bookshop, Rachel had been making comments – subtle suggestions sprinkled through everyday conversations about how Jayna might want to "explore her options" or "take things slow" when Claire was released.

"She doesn't know you like I do," Jayna said finally, the words hanging in the stale prison air. "She hasn't seen what I've seen, hasn't felt what I've felt."

Claire laughed, a short, harsh sound that bounced off the institutional walls. "Maybe she knows me better than you think. Maybe she sees what you don't want to – that I'm just going to drag you back down to where I found you. Back to situations that get out of hand and choices you'll regret."

"That's not true," Jayna insisted, reaching for Claire's hand across the table, needing the physical connection to anchor her. To her shock, Claire pulled away, leaving Jayna's fingers outstretched in the empty space between them.

"Isn't it?" Claire's voice was cold now, a wall of ice between them. "Tell me, Jayna. What do you think is going to happen when I get out? That I'll get some minimum wage job stacking shelves between midnight and dawn? That we'll get a cute little apartment and play house like normal people? That we'll just forget everything that came before?"

"We could," Jayna said, hating how small her voice sounded, how desperate. "We could try. People start over all the time. Why not us?"

Claire shook her head, a strand of hair falling across her face that she didn't bother to push away. "People like us don't get normal, Jay. We get by. We survive. And sometimes that means making tough choices – choices that hurt now but save pain later."

A realisation hit Jayna with the force of a physical blow. "Is this about those plans you mentioned? The ones you've yet to tell me about?"

Claire's expression shuttered, closing like a door slamming in Jayna's face. "It doesn't matter anymore. I don't want to talk about it."

"It matters to me," Jayna pressed, refusing to let it drop.

Claire's silence stretched between them, taut as a wire, and it was answer enough.

Jayna sat back, a hollow feeling opening up in her chest like a sinkhole. "So that's it? You've got some scheme that you know I won't go along with, so now you're cutting me loose? Throwing it all away because I won't risk going back to prison?"

"I'm setting you free," Claire corrected, her voice gentler now, almost tender. "You've got a real shot at something good, Jayna. A life with bookshelves and coffee shops and people who don't suspect you when they meet you. Don't throw it away for me. I'm not worth the sacrifice."

"That's my choice to make," Jayna argued, feeling her magic surge again, stronger this time, responding to the depth of her emotions. "Not yours. Not Rachel's. Mine. I get to decide what I'm willing to risk and who I'm willing to risk it for."

"And I'm making mine," Claire said firmly, squaring her shoulders like she was bracing for a blow. "I think we should split. At least until I get out, figure out what I'm doing. Until we've both had a chance to see what life is like on the outside."

Jayna stared at her in disbelief, feeling like the floor had dropped away beneath her. "Split up? But we've been together for almost two years. We've talked about getting a place together, building a life – we've mapped it out down to the colour of the curtains and the side of the bed we'd each sleep on."

"Prison fantasies," Claire cut in, the words brutal and sharp. "That's all they were. Bedtime stories we told ourselves to make the nights pass faster. They were never going to survive the light of day."

Jayna thought of all the nights they'd whispered to each other after lights out, planning their future together in exquisite detail. All the deep conversations they'd had, promising to wait for each other no matter what. The small gifts exchanged – the silver ring, the dog-eared paperback with notes in the margin. Had it all meant nothing to Claire? Had it all just been a way to pass the time?

"I don't believe you," Jayna said, her voice shaking with emotion she couldn't contain. "I don't believe you want to end things between us. I think you're scared and pushing me away because it's easier than risking failure."

Claire's expression hardened again, the vulnerability disappearing behind her protective walls. "Believe what you want. But I'm done pretending we have some fairytale future waiting for us. We're not characters in one of your books, Jayna. This is real life, and in real life, people like us don't get happy endings."

A guard called out the five-minute warning, his voice echoing in the sparse room.

Claire stood up abruptly, the chair scraping against the floor with a sound that set Jayna's teeth on edge. "Don't visit me next time, ok? I think we both need some space to figure things out."

Jayna remained seated, stunned into immobility, feeling like she'd been caught in a sudden earthquake. "Claire, please... We can work through this. Whatever it is, we can face it together."

But Claire was already turning away, her posture rigid with forced determination. "Take care of yourself, Jayna. I mean that. Don't let anyone or anything pull you back down – especially me."

Jayna watched, frozen in place as Claire walked away to the secure area, not once looking back at the wreckage she'd left behind.

The bus ride home passed in a blur of muted colours and indistinct shapes. Jayna stared out the window, watching the city slide by without really seeing it – the storefronts and pedestrians melting together in a bland wash of movement. Her fingers kept returning to the silver ring Claire had given her, twisting it round and round until the skin beneath started to feel raw.

When she arrived at the apartment, Rachel was in the kitchen, the spicy aroma of her cooking filling the small space with warmth that Jayna couldn't feel. Rachel was chopping vegetables for dinner, the rhythmic sound of the knife against the cutting board stopping abruptly as Jayna entered. One look at Jayna's face, and she put down the knife, wiping her hands on a dishtowel.

"Oh, honey. What happened?" The concern in her voice was genuine, her eyes soft with worry.

The simple question broke the dam Jayna had been holding together by sheer force of will. Her knees buckled beneath her like collapsing scaffolding, and Rachel was there in an instant, guiding her to the sofa, holding her as sobs forced their way through her body.

"She ended it," Jayna managed between gasps for air, her words fractured by grief. "She said… we were kidding ourselves. That we don't have a future. That it was all just fantasy."

Rachel stroked Jayna's hair, making soothing noises that reminded her of childhood fevers and scraped knees. "I'm so sorry, sweetheart. I know how much she meant to you."

"You knew, didn't you?" Jayna pulled back, wiping roughly at her eyes with the heel of her hand. "You saw this coming with those visions of yours. You knew she'd break my heart."

Rachel hesitated, her hands stilling in Jayna's hair, then nodded with reluctance. "I saw possibilities. This was one of them – not the only one, but one that seemed… likely. The future is never certain, just probable."

"Why didn't you warn me?" Jayna demanded, a flash of anger cutting through her grief. "Why let me walk into this blindfolded if you knew what was waiting?"

"Would you have believed me?" Rachel asked gently, her eyes wise with years of navigating the treacherous waters of foresight. "Or would you have just pushed her away faster, trying to prevent something that needed to happen naturally? Sometimes the path to healing requires the wound first."

Jayna had no answer for that, the fight draining out of her as quickly as it had flared. She leaned back against the sofa, emotionally drained, feeling like she'd been hollowed out. "She thinks she'll drag me down. That I'm better off without her pulling me back into old habits and dangerous choices."

"And what do you think?" Rachel asked, her voice careful, neutral.

"I think she's scared," Jayna said. "I think she sees me building a life out here, and she's terrified she won't fit into it. That she'll be the one thing that doesn't belong in the picture I'm painting."

Rachel nodded, her expression thoughtful. "That seems likely. Fear sometimes makes people push away the things they want most. It feels safer than risking rejection later."

"So what do I do now?" Jayna asked, feeling lost in unfamiliar territory, a map with no landmarks. "How do I fix this when she won't even let me try?"

"You keep going," Rachel said simply, her hand warm on Jayna's shoulder. "You keep building that life. And maybe, when Claire gets out and sees what's possible – what you've created for yourself despite everything – you can both figure out if there's still something worth fighting for. Time has a way of changing perspectives."

Jayna stared down at the silver ring, watching the light play across its simple surface. After a long moment, she slipped it off and placed it on the coffee table with deliberate care. The indentation it left on her finger felt strange, exposed – a physical reminder of absence.

"I'm going to take a shower," she said, standing up on legs that still felt unsteady.

"I'll have dinner ready when you're done," Rachel promised, her eyes following her niece with concern. "And Jayna? It's ok to grieve this. Even if it's not forever, it's still a loss. You're allowed to feel everything that comes with that."

Under the hot spray of the shower, steam rising around her like fog, Jayna finally let herself feel everything – the anger that burned like fire, the hurt that cut like glass, the confusion that swirled like autumn leaves in a storm. But beneath it all was something unexpected: a tiny, guilty sense of relief. As if a responsibility she hadn't even realised she'd been carrying had been lifted from her shoulders.

She thought about the book she'd been reading on her breaks at work – a fantasy novel with a protagonist who forged her own path – the community college catalogue she'd been browsing online, the small pleasures of her daily routine that had begun to accumulate like pennies in a jar. None of it erased the pain of losing Claire, but it was something – a life taking shape, day by day, bit by bit.

Chapter Five

Summer bled into autumn, leaves turning from green to gold as Jayna settled deeper into her new life. The bookstore had become a sanctuary, a place where she felt competent and valued. The worn wooden shelves, the comforting scent of paper and binding glue, the quiet murmur of browsers lost in literary worlds – all of it had become as familiar to her as breathing. Eliza had promoted her to assistant manager, entrusting her with opening the shop some mornings and even ordering new inventory. The substantiality of those small responsibilities anchored Jayna in ways she hadn't expected, giving structure to days that had once stretched before her with terrifying emptiness.

On a crisp October afternoon, when the sunlight slanted golden through the shop windows and dust motes danced in the air, Jayna was helping a young woman with electric blue hair select books on herbalism. She'd been explaining the difference between medicinal and culinary approaches when the bell above the door chimed its familiar welcome. She glanced up automatically and froze, her sentence trailing into silence.

Claire stood in the doorway, hands shoved deep in the pockets of a denim jacket that made her look different from how Jayna remembered her – a soft, faded blue that brought out the colour of her eyes. Her hair was longer, styled differently, with gentle waves falling past her shoulders instead of the messy, practical style she'd worn in prison. She'd gained back some of the weight she'd lost, her face fuller and healthier, cheekbones less sharp, the shadows beneath her eyes less pronounced. She looked both achingly familiar and like a stranger.

"Sorry," Claire said, clearly seeing Jayna's shock, a flush creeping into her cheeks. "I should have called first."

Jayna turned back to her customer, her hands slightly trembling as she finished the conversation on autopilot, explaining care instructions for the rare first edition on Alpine herbs that the blue-haired woman had selected. Her voice sounded distant to her own ears, as though coming from down a long corridor. When the transaction was complete, she took a steadying breath before approaching Claire, who stood awkwardly near the doorway, examining a display of local authors with feigned interest.

"You're out," she said stupidly, stating the obvious, the words feeling clumsy on her tongue.

Claire nodded, meeting her eyes briefly before looking away. "Got out last week. Early release for good behaviour." Her fingers fidgeted with a button on her jacket, a nervous gesture Jayna had never seen before.

Jayna did the maths, counting the time in her head. Claire would have had a few more months left on her original sentence. "That's... that's great." The words felt weak, inadequate for the blend of emotions churning inside her.

An awkward silence stretched between them. Around them, customers browsed, oblivious to the tension crackling in the air. A teenage boy flipped through a graphic novel by the window; an elderly woman examined cookbooks with careful deliberation; a couple whispered together over a travel guide to Portugal. The ordinary rhythm of the bookstore continued while Jayna's world tilted on its axis.

"Can we talk?" Claire asked finally, her voice softening with uncertainty. "Maybe after your shift? I'll wait, if that's ok?" She shifted her weight from one foot to the other, a gesture so uncharacteristically hesitant that it made Jayna's chest tighten.

Jayna checked the time on the antique clock above the register, its brass pendulum swinging with comforting regularity. "I get off in an hour."

"I'll go grab a coffee and come back," Claire said, backing towards the door. "If you change your mind, I'll understand." There was an intense vulnerability in her expression that Jayna had rarely seen during their time together, a raw openness that made her look younger, less guarded.

Before Jayna could respond, Claire was gone, the bell jingling in her wake, leaving behind only the faint scent of unfamiliar perfume – something citrusy and clean, nothing like the institutional soap smell that had clung to her during prison visits.

Jayna moved through the rest of her shift in a fog, shelving books in the wrong sections, fumbling with the credit card machine, losing the thread of conversations mid-sentence. Her mind kept replaying Claire's appearance, searching for meaning in every detail – the denim jacket, the different hairstyle, the way she held herself less defensively. When Eliza approached her near the end of her shift, concern etched in the fine lines around her eyes, Jayna managed a smile and blamed her distraction on a headache. Inside, her thoughts were racing like leaves caught in a whirlwind. What did Claire want? Why had she come to the bookstore? And why hadn't she got in touch to say she was being released early?

At five o'clock, as the afternoon light began to fade into evening shadows, Jayna said goodbye to Eliza, who gave her a knowing look, too perceptive by half.

"That woman who came in earlier... she seemed to know you." Eliza's voice was casual, but her eyes were sharp with concern.

Jayna hesitated, her fingers nervously smoothing a wrinkle in her apron. "She's... an old friend."

Eliza's expression softened, the lines around her mouth easing. "Claire?"

Jayna nodded, unable to form words around the lump in her throat.

"Go easy," Eliza advised, patting Jayna's arm with a weathered hand. "On her and on yourself." The older woman's eyes held no judgment, only the wisdom of someone who had witnessed enough in life to know how complicated hearts could be.

Outside the bookstore, the evening had turned cooler, the breeze carrying the scent of fallen leaves and woodsmoke. Claire was waiting, leaning against a wrought-iron lamppost, her face half-illuminated by its glow. She straightened when she saw Jayna, smoothing her hands down her jeans in a nervous gesture.

"You came back," Jayna observed, pulling her cardigan tighter around herself, whether against the chill or as a form of protection, she wasn't sure.

"I said I would." Claire shifted her weight nervously, her boots scuffing against the pavement. "There's a café around the corner. Unless you'd rather not..." She trailed off, leaving room for rejection.

"The café's fine," Jayna said, leading the way down the familiar street, hyper-aware of Claire's presence a few steps behind her. The sound of Claire's footfalls – different now in boots rather than prison-issued shoes – created an odd counterpoint to her own steps.

They settled at a small table by the window at Grounds for Thought, the café where Jayna often came on her lunch breaks. The barista, a tattooed young man named Marco, raised an eyebrow at Jayna's companion but said nothing as he took their orders. Claire ordered a large mocha with extra whipped cream and a shot of caramel – something she had talked about craving constantly in prison, describing it in such detail that Jayna had almost been able to taste it herself. Jayna stuck to plain black coffee, needing its bitter clarity to ground her in this surreal moment.

"You look well," Claire said after their drinks arrived, her fingers curling around the oversized ceramic mug as though absorbing its warmth. "Still with the purple hair, I see. It suits you." Her gaze travelled over Jayna's face with a hunger that suggested she was memorising details, taking note of changes.

Jayna ran a hand through her hair, freshly dyed again just last week. "Thanks. You look... different." The word felt insufficient for the changes she was witnessing.

Claire smiled slightly, a dimple appearing in her left cheek. "Good different or bad different?"

"Just different," Jayna replied, not ready to admit that Claire looked better than she'd ever seen her – healthier, calmer, her eyes clearer and more focused, like someone who had finally emerged from a long illness. "Why didn't you tell me you were getting out early?" The question had been burning inside her since Claire appeared in the bookstore doorway.

Claire cradled her drink, the mountain of whipped cream slowly dissolving into the chocolate beneath. "I wasn't sure you'd want to know. After the way things ended…" Her voice trailed off, laden with unspoken regrets.

"You mean after you ended things," Jayna corrected, unable to keep the edge from her voice, the old hurt rising to the surface like a bruise being pressed.

Claire winced, her shoulders hunching slightly. "I deserved that." She took a deep breath, her chest rising and falling beneath the denim jacket. "I owe you an explanation. And an apology." Her fingers traced the rim of her mug, leaving smudges in the foam.

Jayna said nothing, waiting, the silence between them punctuated by the hiss of the espresso machine and the murmur of conversations at nearby tables.

"I was scared," Claire admitted finally, the words seeming to cost her something. "Watching you build this new life on the outside while I was still stuck in there… it was harder than I expected. Every phone call, you'd have these new stories – about the bookstore, about staying with Rachel, about making friends. And I'd have nothing new to share except which guard was being a problem that week or what fight broke out in the yard." She swallowed hard. "I started to convince myself that I'd just mess everything up for you when I got out."

"So instead of talking to me about it, you pushed me away." Jayna's voice was flat, but her hands betrayed her emotions as she gripped her coffee cup.

Claire took a deep breath before speaking, her fingers wrapped tightly around her mug as she stared down into the dark liquid. She seemed to consider her words carefully, as if trying to find a way to make them sound less like a confession and more like an explanation.

"You know," she began, her voice a little hesitant, "before everything fell apart, I had this... stupid plan." She gave a short, rueful laugh. "It was with someone inside – she arrived after you'd left. We were going to run a telemarketing scam, using contraband phones to make calls. All sorts of illegal stuff... I know, it was reckless. Dangerous."

Jayna didn't say anything, her heart clenching at the thought of Claire being caught up in something like that. Claire kept her eyes on her mug, her thumb tracing the edge, as if it helped steady her.

"When I broke things off with you, I told myself it was because I couldn't drag you down with me. But honestly, I think it was just easier to push you away than admit I was spiralling. I wasn't thinking straight – hadn't been for a while." Claire's voice dropped to a murmur, as though the truth of the situation embarrassed her. "That's when I started the counselling," she said, her tone softening. "At first, I thought it might just end up being a waste of time. But then… I was sent to see a clinical psychologist and they diagnosed me with bipolar disorder. It felt like a punch to the gut, to be honest. But then it made sense – all those highs and lows, the impulsive decisions. I always thought I was just broken or weak. But this, this gave me a way to understand it."

Jayna felt her pulse quicken, the rush of relief mixed with something else – something like grief. She had always known Claire was more than her impulsive decisions, but hearing this... it was like seeing her for the first time again. Different. Maybe better. But also so far away from the Claire she remembered.

"The meds, the therapy..." Claire continued, finally looking up to meet Jayna's gaze, "...it's helped. A lot. I can think clearer now, Jayna. And maybe more importantly, I can stop myself before I do something stupid. That's why I got out early. They saw the progress, and they figured I'd improved enough to stay out of trouble. I didn't mean to hurt you when I broke things off with you. I told myself I was doing it for you, but really I was protecting myself. From disappointment. From rejection." The admission hung between them, raw with honesty.

Jayna took a sip of her coffee, the bitterness coating her tongue. Claire chewed anxiously on her lower lip, a strand of hair falling across her face. She tucked it behind her ear with fingers that trembled slightly.

"I was wrong to hurt you like that. I owe you an apology." Claire hesitated, uncertainty clouding her features. "But mostly I wanted to see you. To make sure you're ok."

"I'm ok," Jayna said, surprised to find she meant it. "I'm glad you've opened up to me. And I'm glad you got the help you needed. None of this changes how much I care about you."

Claire's throat bobbed as she swallowed hard, her eyes flicking to look away. "I wasn't sure you'd still want to talk to me after hearing all that. I pushed you away. I was selfish."

"Perhaps you needed to be. You did something really hard. You faced yourself."

Claire let out a slow breath, rolling her mug between her palms. Then, after a pause, she looked up, her gaze steady, searching. "Anyway," she said. "How are you, Jayna? Really."

It wasn't just a polite question, something to fill the space between them. Claire meant it. She always had a way of cutting through the surface, of asking in a way that made it clear she actually wanted the answer.

Jayna hesitated, not because she didn't know what to say, but because the truth felt so different from anything she would have expected a year ago. "I'm... ok," she said, still surprised by how much she meant it. "Better, actually."

Claire raised an eyebrow, prompting her to go on.

Jayna exhaled, rubbing her thumb absently over the rim of her cup. "I think – no, I know – I used to carry so much anger. About the way people looked at me. About the way I grew up. About how unfair everything felt. And I let it fester." She glanced at Claire, her lips twitching into something like a self-deprecating smile. "And, let's be real, I let it fuel my worst decisions."

Claire didn't argue. She didn't need to. They both knew the truth of it.

"But prison... and then moving in with Rachel... I don't know... It made me see how pointless that anger was. Not that it wasn't justified," she added quickly. "But holding on to it, feeding it until I burned myself up inside? It wasn't worth it. None of it was worth losing control the way I used to."

Claire's gaze sharpened, understanding flickering there. "Your magic," she said.

Jayna nodded. "Yeah. It's not that I don't feel things anymore. I do. But I don't let myself get so angry that I use it just because I want someone to feel as bad as I do. I don't want to be that person anymore." She met Claire's eyes. "And I think... I think I finally believe I don't have to be."

Claire was quiet for a moment, watching Jayna like she was seeing someone new. Then, she gave a small, almost wistful smile. "I always knew you had it in you," she murmured.

Jayna huffed a soft laugh. "Yeah? Well, it took me a while to figure it out."

Claire shook her head. "Doesn't matter how long it takes. Just matters that you got there. I'm happy for you."

"I've learnt a lot about myself," Jayna said carefully, choosing her words with precision. "About what I want. What I need. And yes, some of that happened because you pushed me away. But that doesn't mean I didn't miss you." The admission cost her something – a piece of the armour she'd built around herself during these months of separation.

Hope flickered in Claire's eyes, lighting them from within.

"So what now?" Jayna asked. "What do you want?"

"Honestly? I don't know." Claire laughed, a self-deprecating sound that broke some of the tension. "I've got a place to stay – my cousin Tara's letting me crash on her couch until I find something permanent. She's got this tiny apartment over in Riverdale, not much, but it's clean and she doesn't ask too many questions. I've got a job interview tomorrow at a furniture restoration place. The guy who runs it is friends with my parole officer, so he's willing to give me a chance. Turns out all that time in the prison workshop actually taught me something useful."

"That's great," Jayna said. She could picture Claire working with her hands, bringing old pieces of furniture back to life, her natural dexterity finding purpose in detailed work.

"But beyond that..." Claire met Jayna's eyes directly, her gaze steady. "I miss you. I miss us. The way you always sang off-key in the shower. The way you'd get so excited about a new book that you'd read whole paragraphs out loud to me. The way you always saw more in me than I saw in myself." She paused, swallowing hard. "But I also understand if that door is closed now."

Jayna thought long and hard for a moment. The pain of Claire's rejection, sharp as broken glass at first, had gradually dulled to an ache she could live with. She had slowly built a life without her – finding rhythms to her days, developing new friendships, discovering parts of herself that had been overshadowed by the intensity of their relationship. And then there was the silver ring, now sitting in a small box on her dressing table, neither worn nor discarded.

"Maybe we need to get to know each other again," she said finally. "The new versions of us."

Claire's expression brightened, hope blooming across her features like a sunrise. "I'd like that."

"As friends," Jayna clarified, needing to establish this boundary for her own protection. "At least for now. I need time, Claire. Time to figure out what I want, what's best for me. For us."

Claire nodded, accepting this limitation without argument. "Friends. I can do that." She hesitated, picking at a loose thread on the sleeve of her jacket. "Does that mean I can call you sometime? Maybe we could grab dinner next week?"

Jayna smiled. "Yeah. I'd like that."

They finished their coffees, the conversation shifting to lighter topics – Claire's amazement at how many new shops had opened during her incarceration, Jayna's stories about eccentric bookstore customers who insisted on detailed recommendations for books they would never read, the stray cat that had adopted the bookstore and slept in the window display. The tension between them eased gradually, making space for moments of their old, easy rapport to shine through.

When they finally stepped outside, the autumn evening was settling over the city, street lamps flickering to life along the tree-lined avenue. The air had grown even cooler.

Claire shuffled her feet on the pavement, scuffing the toe of her boot against a crack in the concrete. "Well, I guess I'll head home now. It was nice catching up with you. I think I'll…"

"Wait," Jayna interrupted, rummaging through her bag for her phone. "Give me your number so I can reach you about that dinner."

Claire recited her cousin's landline number, watching as Jayna entered it into her contacts, the screen illuminating her face with a soft blue glow.

"I'll call you," Jayna promised, tucking the phone away.

"I'll be waiting," Claire replied, a hint of her old cockiness returning in the slight upward tilt of her chin and the half-smile that Jayna had once found irresistible. She shoved her hands into her pockets and nodded towards the opposite street. "My bus is that way." She gave Jayna one last look before turning and heading to the bus stop that would take her across the city to where she was staying.

As Jayna walked home, she felt lighter somehow, as though a weight she'd been carrying had shifted, becoming more balanced. She didn't feel healed – there were still too many complicated feelings for that – but hopeful, perhaps.

Chapter Six

The late January night was bitterly cold, the kind that made even the hardiest city dwellers hurry from one heated space to another with hunched shoulders and buried chins. A merciless wind sliced through the concrete corridors between buildings, carrying the promise of snow that had yet to materialise. Jayna stood outside Voltage nightclub. She hadn't been here since the night of her almost-fight. The memory felt simultaneously distant and fresh, like a photograph that had faded at the edges but retained its vivid centre.

Music thumped through the walls, a persistent beat. The bass notes seemed to synchronise with her own quickened pulse. The line of people waiting to get in stamped their feet and huddled together against the cold, their collective breath forming a cloud of condensation that hung in the frigid air. Through the glass doors, Jayna could see the familiar crowded bar, the hypnotic flashing lights, the press of bodies moving in rhythmic abandon, oblivious to the world outside.

"You sure about this?" Claire asked, standing beside her, her voice carrying the gentle concern that had become characteristic of their rebuilt relationship. "We could go somewhere quieter. Maybe that bar you mentioned last week?"

Jayna shook her head, her purple hair catching the glow of the neon sign above them. "I've missed this place. I want to start enjoying it again now that I know I can control myself." She paused, running her gloved fingers over the textured surface of her coat. "Full circle, you know?"

Claire squeezed her hand, the pressure reassuring through their gloves. "Your call. But if anyone spills a drink on you, I'm not breaking up the fight. I like being on the outside too much." Her attempt at lightness couldn't quite mask the seriousness beneath – they both knew what freedom meant now, in a way they hadn't been able to appreciate before.

Jayna laughed, the sound crystallising in the cold air. "Don't worry. We've got this." The understatement hung between them, acknowledging how far they had both come.

After leaving their coats with the cloakroom attendant at the entrance, they made their way through the crowded club to the bar. Bodies pressed against them from all sides, the air thick with perfume, cologne, and the unmistakable scent of spilt alcohol. The same bartender from that tension-fuelled night was working, his deft hands mixing drinks with confidence, though he showed no sign of recognising Jayna among the sea of faces demanding his attention.

"Rum and coke, please," Jayna requested, her voice raised to carry over the music. "And a cranberry vodka for my friend." The word felt simultaneously inadequate and cautious – the perfect encapsulation of where they stood.

Claire raised an eyebrow at the "friend" designation but said nothing, her expression a mixture of amusement and something more complex. Three months of careful rebuilding had brought them to a place of comfortable familiarity, but they were still navigating the boundaries of their new relationship with deliberate steps. Friends, yes, but with the history and connection of something deeper simmering beneath the surface, an undercurrent that neither of them could fully ignore.

They found a small table in the corner, away from the worst of the noise and the constant traffic of dancers heading to and from the floor. The sticky surface bore the rings of countless drinks, the scars of countless nights like this one. Claire looked good tonight – her hair coloured chestnut with blonde highlights and styled in loose waves that caught the intermittent light, her curves accentuated by a deep green sweater dress that complemented her skin tone, making her stand out even in the shifting light. The job at the furniture restoration shop had worked out well, giving her both the stability and creative satisfaction she'd never admitted to craving during their time inside. She had moved from her cousin's couch to a small studio apartment across the city, sparse in furnishings but unmistakably hers in the careful arrangement of the few possessions she valued.

"So," Claire said, leaning in to be heard over the relentless thrum of the music, her perfume – something new, with notes of sandalwood and vanilla – momentarily displacing the club's more chaotic scents. "Why the trip down memory lane? Special occasion?"

"Just keen to celebrate how far we've both come," Jayna said with a smile.

"I'll drink to that," Claire said, looking more at ease with herself than Jayna had ever seen her.

They clinked glasses, the sound lost in the club's noise but the gesture meaningful nonetheless. Jayna felt a familiar warmth spreading through her that had nothing to do with the alcohol and everything to do with connection. Over the past three months, she'd rediscovered all the things she'd first loved about Claire – her dry humour that could cut through tension like a knife, her fierce loyalty to the few she allowed close, her surprisingly tender heart beneath the tough exterior cultivated through years of necessity. But she'd also discovered new things: Claire's determination to stay on the right path despite the constant pull of old habits, her passion for furniture restoration that bordered on reverence, the way she now thought before she acted, considering consequences with a maturity that had been absent before.

There was no denying the reality – bipolar disorder wasn't something that could be conquered once and for all, neatly wrapped up and left behind. There would always be the risk of bad days, of spirals, of moments when it all might push Claire towards old, destructive impulses. But now, she had something she didn't have before: knowledge. A name for the chaos that had once ruled her life, a treatment plan that gave her a fighting chance, and the unwavering desire to try.

And that mattered more than anything.

Claire wasn't promising perfection – Jayna wouldn't have believed her if she had. But what she *was* promising, in her own way, was stability where there had once been uncertainty. A future shaped not by reckless instinct but by understanding and choice. And as Jayna looked at her now, at the quiet confidence in her posture and the steady light in her eyes, she believed in that future too.

"Dance with me?" Claire asked suddenly, nodding towards the crowded dance floor where bodies moved in various states of rhythm and abandon, illuminated by flashing lights that painted everyone in momentary blues, reds, and purples.

Jayna hesitated, a reflexive caution born of months of careful boundary-setting, then nodded, surprising herself with how much she wanted this simple connection. They abandoned their half-finished drinks and pushed their way through the crowd, navigating the press of bodies. The music was loud, some pulsing electronic beat with a female vocalist whose words were lost in the mix, reduced to emotional phonetics that nonetheless communicated something primal and urgent.

Claire slipped an arm around Jayna's waist, pulling her close but not too close, always respectful of the boundaries Jayna had established in their new relationship. The touch was firm enough to be intentional but light enough to be broken if desired – a perfect embodiment of where they stood.

They moved together, remembering a rhythm they'd discovered long ago in the prison recreation yard, dancing to music only they could hear during the few precious minutes of free time. Back then, they'd had to be careful, subtle, their movements constrained by both space and scrutiny. Now, they could move freely, Jayna's purple hair catching the flashing lights as she spun, her body responding to the music with a liberation that felt both foreign and familiar.

"I've missed this," Claire said into Jayna's ear.

Jayna smiled, saying nothing but allowing herself to move closer, her hand finding Claire's shoulder, their bodies synchronising to the beat with a naturalness that spoke of deeper connection. In that moment, all the complications fell away – the past with its mistakes and regrets, the struggles of re-entry into a world that rarely made space for second chances, the careful distance they'd maintained since reconnecting. There was only the music, the movement, the electricity between them that had never fully dissipated, despite everything.

As the song transitioned to something slower, more intimate, the crowd around them shifted, some departing for drinks, others drawing closer to partners. Claire's hand slid to the small of Jayna's back, a question in the gesture. "Is this ok?" she murmured, her voice barely audible over the music but her meaning clear.

Jayna nodded, resting her head against Claire's shoulder, breathing in the familiar scent of her – that same underlying essence that not even prison soap had been able to mask, now enhanced with subtle perfume. They swayed together, barely moving, an island of stillness in the chaotic flood of the club.

"I need to tell you something," Claire said softly, her lips close to Jayna's ear.

Jayna pulled back enough to see Claire's face. "What is it?"

"I'm moving."

Jayna froze, her body suddenly rigid against Claire's, the word triggering a cascade of emotions – fear, abandonment, the dread of loss – that surprised her with their intensity. "Moving? Where?" The question emerged more sharply than intended, edged with panic.

"Not far," Claire said quickly, her hand making soothing circles on Jayna's back. "Just to the west side. I got offered a better job at this high-end furniture place, restoring antiques. The owner saw my work at a client's house and tracked me down." There was a pride in her voice that couldn't be hidden, a legitimate excitement for recognition of her talent.

Relief washed over Jayna, the tension draining from her shoulders as quickly as it had appeared. "That's amazing, Claire! Congratulations." The sincerity in her voice was absolute; despite their complicated history, Jayna wanted nothing more than to see Claire succeed, to build the life she deserved.

"Thanks." Claire bit her lip, a gesture of uncertainty that transported Jayna back to their first tentative conversations in the prison yard, before they really knew each other, when everything was possibility. "But there's more. The new place... it's bigger. A one-bedroom instead of just a studio."

"That's great," Jayna said, not quite understanding Claire's nervousness, the significance behind her words still unclear.

"It's very spacious. There's room for one more." Claire's eyes held Jayna's, meaningful, intent, the flashing lights of the club reflected in their depths.

Understanding dawned, a slow sunrise that illuminated everything in a different light. "Are you asking me to move in with you?" The question was direct; Jayna couldn't bear the suspense any longer.

Claire shook her head quickly, her hair catching the light. "No, not exactly. I know that's too much, too soon. I'm just saying... there's room. If you ever wanted to stay over sometimes. Or... eventually... more than sometimes." The careful phrasing revealed how much thought she'd given this, how consciously she was trying to respect Jayna's need for space while still expressing her own desires.

Jayna felt her heartbeat quicken, a flutter of both anxiety and possibility. "Claire..."

"You don't have to answer now," Claire interrupted, her words coming faster now, a rush to clarify. "It's not an ultimatum or anything. Just... something to think about. For the future. Our future, maybe." The last words were tentative, a question as much as a statement.

The song ended, transitioning back to something fast and intense, a jarring shift that mirrored Jayna's internal state. Around them, dancers jumped and thrashed to the new beat, but Jayna and Claire remained still, lost in their private moment as if enclosed in a bubble that the outside world couldn't penetrate.

"I need some air," Jayna said finally, the club's atmosphere suddenly too close, too loud, too much.

Navigating through the packed dance floor, collecting their coats, and moving past the line still waiting to enter, they made their way outside. The cold night air hit them hard, a shock after the heated club. Jayna took deep breaths, her mind racing with possibilities, fears, hopes – all the complexities she hadn't allowed herself to imagine in concrete terms.

"I'm sorry if I freaked you out," Claire said, rubbing her arms against the cold, her breath forming clouds in the frozen air. "I shouldn't have sprung that on you."

"No, it's ok," Jayna assured her, reaching out to touch Claire's arm briefly. "It's just... a lot to process."

The understatement made Claire smile slightly, acknowledging the enormity of what had been proposed. She nodded, understanding in her eyes. "Take all the time you need. I meant what I said – it's not an ultimatum." She shifted from foot to foot, partly from the cold and partly from the lingering tension of vulnerability. "The offer stands, whenever you're ready. If you're ever ready."

Jayna looked at Claire – really looked at her, peeling away the layers of their complicated history to see the woman standing before her. The person she'd fallen for in prison was still there, in the set of her jaw, in the directness of her gaze that refused to be intimidated. But there was also someone new, someone who had faced her demons and chosen a different path. Someone who, like Jayna, had found her way forward through the uncertain terrain of freedom.

"I've got something for you," Jayna said suddenly, reaching into the pocket of her coat, her fingers closing around the small box she'd been carrying all evening, waiting for the right moment. She pulled it out, the black velvet soft against her palm.

Claire stared at it, her eyes widening slightly. "What's that?"

"Open it."

With slightly shaking hands, Claire took the box and opened it. Inside was the silver ring she'd given Jayna in prison, the small amethyst catching the streetlight and reflecting it back in purple flashes. The sight of it seemed to steal Claire's breath, a small gasp escaping her.

"My ring," she said softly, her voice barely audible over the distant traffic and the muffled music from the club.

"I kept it," Jayna explained, watching Claire's face carefully. "Even after everything. I couldn't bring myself to throw it away." She didn't need to elaborate on "everything"; the ring had witnessed it all.

Claire looked up, confusion clouding her features. "Are you... giving it back to me?"

"No," Jayna said firmly, certainty ringing in her voice. "I'm giving it to you. The difference matters."

Claire's brow furrowed, the subtle lines appearing between her eyebrows that Jayna had once traced with a gentle finger in a rare moment of prison privacy. "I don't understand."

"You gave me this ring as a promise – that we'd wait for each other, that we'd be together when we got out." Jayna took the ring from the box, the metal cool against her fingers. "Now I'm giving it to you as a different kind of promise. That we'll keep doing what we've been doing these past few months – getting to know each other again, building something real, something that works on the outside."

Understanding dawned in Claire's eyes, a light that transformed her entire face. "A fresh start."

"Exactly." Jayna held out the ring, offering it like a new beginning. "So what do you say?"

Claire extended her hand, her fingers trembling slightly, and definitely not just from the cold. Jayna slipped the ring onto her finger, the silver band sliding into place as if it had been waiting for this moment. It fitted perfectly, as if the intervening months had changed nothing – at least in this small detail.

"Yes," Claire whispered, the word forming a cloud in the frigid air between them. "To whatever this is, to wherever it's going. Yes."

Before Jayna could respond, a familiar sensation seized her body – an abrupt, sharp tug behind her navel that felt as if someone had hooked a thread into her core and yanked it through a void. A disorientating whirl of light and pressure enveloped her, her stomach twisting painfully as though it was being pulled in multiple directions at once. The very fabric of reality seemed to bend and warp around them, the air thickening, melting, and then, in an instant, everything shifted. The sensation was like being compressed from all sides, her body flickering between states of existence as the world around them fractured and realigned.

And then, as suddenly as it had begun, the chaos stopped.

Jayna stumbled slightly, her legs unsteady as she felt solid ground underfoot again. She was no longer standing on the cold, hard pavement of the club's exterior but was instead in Rachel's living room. Claire was beside her, looking utterly bewildered, her eyes wide and unfocused as she swayed for a moment, her balance momentarily compromised by the sudden teleportation.

"What the hell?!" Claire demanded, her voice still trembling from the residual disorientation. She staggered slightly, one hand shooting out instinctively to steady herself against a nearby bookshelf, her fingers curling around the edge for support. Her eyes flickered around the room as though trying to make sense of what had just happened.

Rachel was sitting on the sofa, a leather-bound book in her lap and a cup of tea steaming on the coffee table – almost exactly as she had been that night when she'd pulled Jayna from potential trouble. Except this time, she looked mortified, her eyes wide with the realisation of what she'd inadvertently done.

"Oh my god, I'm so sorry," Rachel blurted, closing her book with a snap and setting it aside. "I didn't mean... I was just checking in, and I saw you outside the club, and I got confused for a moment – muscle memory, I guess..." Her hands fluttered in explanation, her usual composure completely absent.

Jayna burst out laughing, the absurdity of the situation hitting her all at once. "You teleported us home? Seriously?" The laughter felt cleansing, releasing tension she hadn't noticed she'd been carrying.

"I panicked!" Rachel defended herself, a flush creeping up her neck and into her cheeks. "I saw you outside that club, and for a moment I thought..." She glanced at Claire, who was still trying to get her bearings, taking in the unfamiliar surroundings with cautious curiosity. "I'm Rachel, by the way. Jayna's aunt. This isn't exactly how I planned to meet you."

"Claire," Claire replied faintly, straightening her dress. "Nice to... materialise in your living room." Despite the surreal nature of the introduction, there was a hint of humour in her voice, a resilience that Jayna had always admired.

Jayna couldn't stop laughing, the sound filling the cosy living room. "Rachel, I wasn't in trouble. We were just talking."

"I realise that now," Rachel said, clearly embarrassed, running a hand through her hair. "I'm still getting used to the idea that you can handle yourself. Old habits." She stood up, smoothing her pyjama bottoms with a distracted motion. "I can send you back if you like? It's no trouble at all. I'll just need to..."

"No," Jayna said, surprising herself with the certainty in her voice. "Actually, now that we're here..." She looked at Claire, seeking confirmation. "Maybe it's time you two properly met."

Rachel's eyebrows rose, understanding the significance of the moment. "Are you sure? I don't want to intrude on your evening."

"I'm sure." Jayna took Claire's hand, the gesture deliberate, marking a milestone in their careful rebuilding. "Unless you'd rather go back to the club?"

Claire squeezed her hand, warmth and understanding in the pressure. "No, this is good. Better than good." She smiled at Rachel, the initial shock of teleportation fading into genuine curiosity. "I've heard a lot about you. Your teleportation skills live up to the hype."

Rachel laughed, visibly relaxing, her shoulders dropping from their tense position. "Let me make you both some tea. Or I have wine, if you prefer?"

"Wine would be great," Jayna said, the evening taking an unexpected but not unwelcome turn.

As Rachel went to the kitchen, the sound of cabinet doors opening and glasses clinking drifting back to them, Claire looked around the living room, taking in the spell books stacked on every available surface, the strange artefacts that defied easy categorisation, the comfortable clutter that made it a home. Her gaze lingered on a crystal sphere that pulsed with soft blue light, then moved to a shelf of dried herbs labelled in Rachel's precise handwriting.

"So this is where you live," she said softly, the words carrying significance beyond their simple meaning.

"For now," Jayna replied, letting the implication settle between them, an acknowledgment of Claire's earlier offer without a direct response. "It's been a good place to figure things out."

Rachel returned with wine glasses, a bottle of rich red wine cradled in her arm, and the three of them settled in the living room – Rachel in her favourite armchair, Jayna and Claire on the worn but comfortable sofa, close but not quite touching. To Jayna's relief, the conversation flowed easily, initial awkwardness dissolving into genuine connection. Claire charmed Rachel with stories from the restoration shop, her hands animated as she described bringing forgotten pieces back to life. Rachel, in turn, shared embarrassing tales from Jayna's childhood that had Claire in stitches, her laughter filling the space with warmth.

"She's always been stubborn," Rachel confirmed, her eyes twinkling with affection. "Even as a little girl. Once she decided something, that was it. She always acted as if the world might as well adapt to her because she certainly wasn't going to budge."

"I can imagine," Claire said, her eyes finding Jayna's, the shared history between them giving the simple words layers of meaning.

Later, as the evening wound down, the wine bottle empty and the conversation having traversed everything from furniture restoration techniques to magical theory,

Rachel tactfully excused herself to bed with a gentle touch to Jayna's shoulder as she passed. The gesture spoke volumes – approval, acceptance, trust – leaving Jayna and Claire alone in the living room, the soft lamplight creating shadows that danced on the walls.

"I like her," Claire said, her posture more relaxed now, one leg tucked underneath her on the sofa. "She's nothing like I imagined."

"What did you imagine?" Jayna asked, curious about the picture Claire had formed from her limited prison descriptions.

"I don't know. Someone stricter. More judgmental." Claire shrugged, the movement elegant despite its casualness. "I thought she'd hate me on principle."

"Rachel doesn't hate anyone on principle," Jayna said, thinking of her aunt's boundless capacity for understanding. "She sees possibilities, not fixed outcomes."

Claire nodded, thoughtful, twirling the stem of her empty wine glass between her fingers. "I get why you love her."

They sat in comfortable silence for a moment, the events of the night settling upon them. Outside, a siren wailed briefly before fading into the distance, a reminder of the city continuing its nightly rhythm beyond their temporary sanctuary.

"So," Claire said finally, setting her glass down on the coffee table with deliberate care. "This wasn't exactly how I planned tonight would go."

"No?" Jayna smiled, a slight teasing note in her voice. "What did you have in mind?"

"Well, after the club, I thought maybe a quiet walk by the river. Then I'd walk you home, maybe kiss you goodnight at the door..." Claire's voice grew softer, more intimate, the words carrying a gentle heat. "Maybe you'd invite me in."

"That sounds nice," Jayna admitted, imagining the scenario – the glow of streetlights on water, their breath mingling in the cold air, the anticipation of a threshold crossed. "But so is this." She gestured around them, at the comfortable room with its magical artefacts and well-worn furniture.

"Being here, with you. With Rachel. It feels right somehow."

"Full circle," Claire agreed, her gaze warm on Jayna's face. "From that night when she yanked you away from trouble at the club."

"Except this time, I wasn't in trouble."

"No," Claire said, her eyes reflecting the lamplight. "This time, you're exactly where you're supposed to be."

Jayna leaned in, closing the distance between them with deliberate slowness, giving Claire every opportunity to pull back. The kiss was gentle at first, exploratory, a relearning of familiar territory that had changed in subtle ways. Then deeper – months of careful restraint giving way to something more urgent, more honest. When they finally pulled apart, both slightly breathless, Jayna rested her forehead against Claire's.

"Stay," she whispered, the word both a request and an offer. "Tonight. We'll figure out the rest tomorrow."

Claire nodded, her fingers tracing Jayna's cheek with feather-light touches, as if memorising the contours. "Tomorrow. And all the days after that."

As they settled together on the sofa, Claire's head on Jayna's shoulder, Jayna's arm around Claire's waist, Jayna thought about the journey that had brought them here. From prison cells to freedom, from loss to rediscovery, from panic to something approaching balance. The path had been neither straight nor easy, marked by setbacks and moments of doubt that had threatened to derail everything. It hadn't been easy, and it wouldn't always be easy going forward. But for the first time, Jayna wasn't anxious about the future, wasn't counting down days or setting arbitrary milestones for happiness.

She had her job at the bookstore, with its quiet rhythms and the satisfaction of connecting readers with stories that might change their lives. She had respect for *when and how* to use her magic, understanding that it wasn't a tool for every emotional storm or instant desire. Magic, she had learnt, demanded respect – not just for its power but for the balance it required. It wasn't something to be wielded on impulse, no matter how emotionally overwhelming the moment, but something to be carefully considered, measured, and used only when truly necessary. She had her relationship with Rachel, no longer defined by dependency but by mutual respect and shared magical heritage.

And now, perhaps, she had a new chapter with Claire – not a continuation of their prison romance, with all its intensity and limitations, but something healthier, more solid. Built on choice rather than circumstance, on understanding rather than escape, on seeing each other clearly rather than through the distorting lens of confinement.

Outside, the city continued its nighttime pulse, lights aglow in windows across the skyline, each representing lives unfolding in their own complex patterns. Inside, Jayna watched the silver ring glinting on Claire's finger as she dozed against her shoulder, her breathing deep and even. Same ring, new promise. Same hearts, different women.

Full circle, but further along the spiral. Not an ending, but a beginning built on everything that had come before, the foundation stronger for having been tested, rebuilt, reinforced.

Jayna closed her eyes, feeling the steady rhythm of Claire's breathing beside her, the warmth of her body a tangible reminder of presence, of connection. She wasn't counting down the days to something better, nor escaping into fantasies of a different life. She was simply here, content in the present moment.